The Snowman

Raymond Briggs

A few words from
Raymond Briggs

THE SNOWMAN has become a world-wide phenomenon. The book is published in over fifteen countries and has been in print for over thirty years. The film has been shown on television every Christmas for the last quarter of a century. Now, the musical, staged annually, continues beyond its tenth year. There are hundreds of items of merchandise, mostly in Japan but all over the world, too. Dozens of Japanese businessmen are walking about in socks with my signature running up their legs! Why, for heaven's sake?

The book won awards in this country, including one from the V&A, as well as others in Holland, Italy and America. The film won a BAFTA in Britain and was nominated for an Oscar in America. Then, despite the wonders of computer-generated imagery, this old-fashioned, hand-drawn film has survived and is still held in great affection by everyone.

At signing sessions, middle-aged couples come up with their children and say, "We had this book when we were children, and now our children are having the same book!" This must be the greatest compliment a writer can receive. If a book can cross one generation like that, there is no reason why it should not cross more.

Now with this new edition, Puffin is making sure that *The Snowman* can continue long beyond the author's lifetime, and I think that's bloomin' marvellous.

Raymond Briggs

PUFFIN BOOKS
Published by the Penguin Group: London, New York, Australia, Canada, India,
Ireland, New Zealand and South Africa
Penguin Books Ltd, Registered Offices: 80 Strand, London WC2R 0RL, England
puffinbooks.com
First published by Hamish Hamilton 1978
Published in Puffin Books 1980
This edition with new introduction published 2011
003 – 10 9 8 7 6 5 4 3
Copyright © Raymond Briggs, 1978, 2011
All rights reserved
The moral right of the author/illustrator has been asserted
Made and printed in China
ISBN: 978–0–141–34009–8

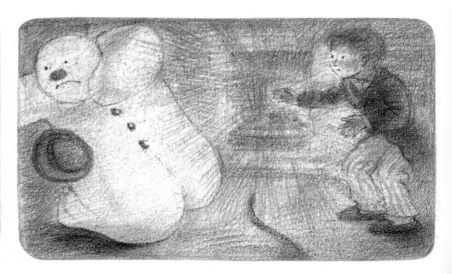

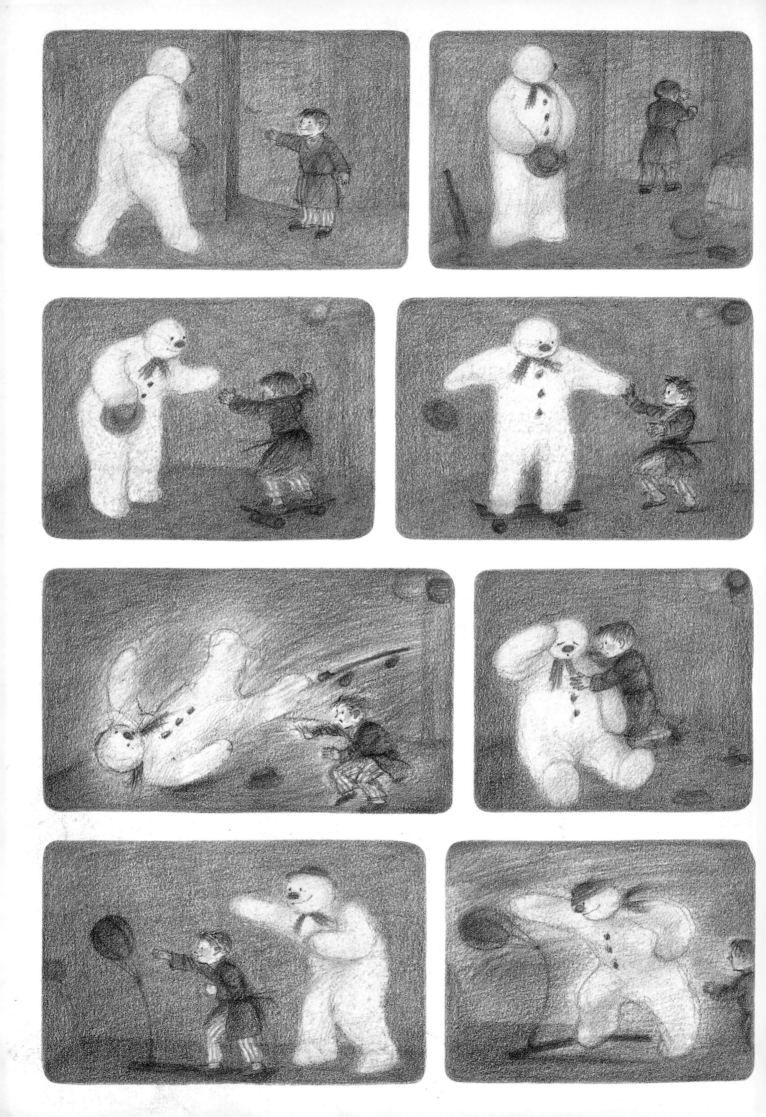

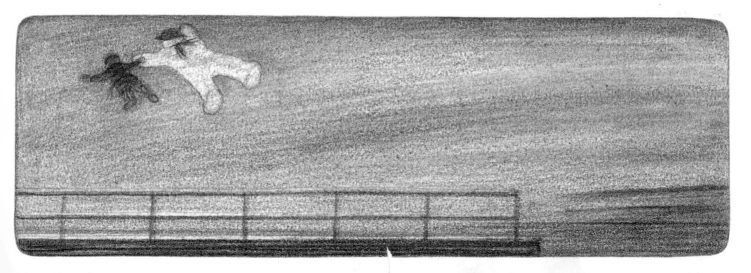

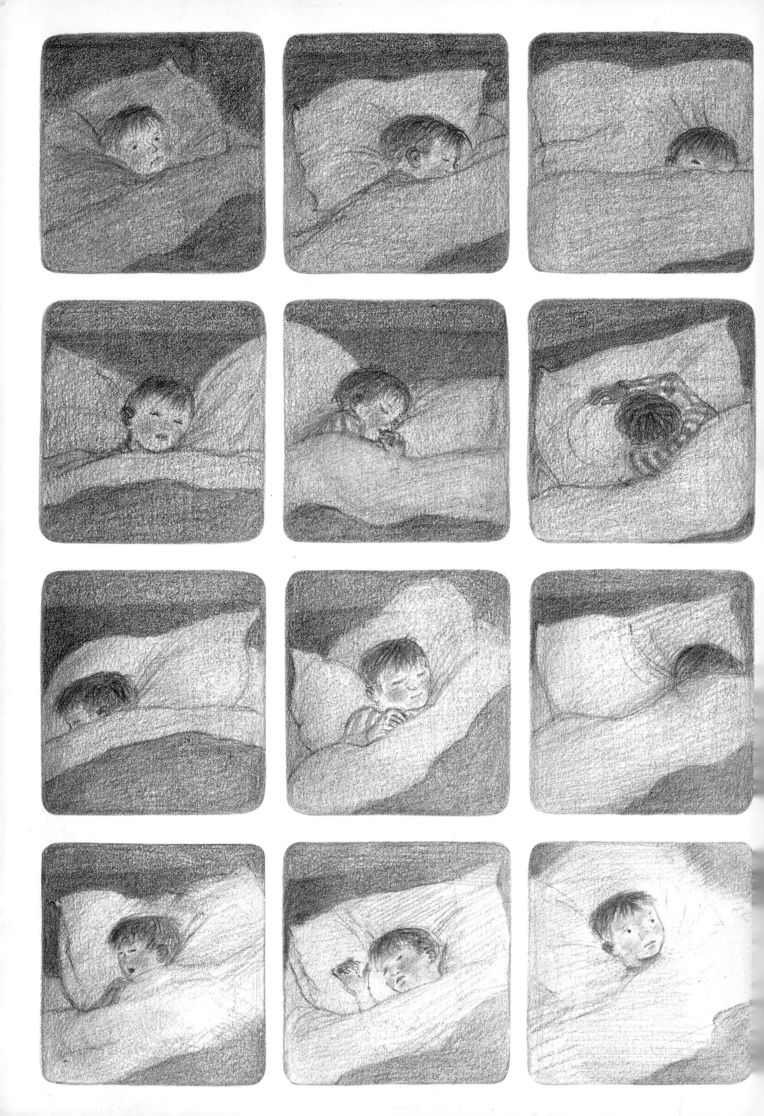